P9-AZW-096

Books by Matt Christopher

Mystery Coach

Mystery Coach

by Matt Christopher

Illustrated by Harvey Kidder

Little, Brown and Company

BOSTON   TORONTO

SECOND PRINTING

T 04/73

Library of Congress Cataloging in Publication Data

Christopher, Matthew F
  Mystery coach.

  SUMMARY: When their coach becomes ill and their
baseball team starts falling apart, several of the
Blazers begin receiving coaching tips from an
anonymous phone caller.
  [1. Baseball--Stories] I. Kidder, Harvey,
illus. II. Title.
PZ7.C458My   [Fic]   72-11924
ISBN 0-316-13955-6

Published simultaneously in Canada
by Little, Brown & Company (Canada) Limited

PRINTED IN THE UNITED STATES OF AMERICA

to
Florence Kramer

Mystery Coach

1

CHRIS RICHARDS stood near second base, wondering if the Blazers were going to have a team or fall apart before the season started.

He lifted his eyeglasses, scratched the bridge of his nose, and let them drop in place again. He didn't feel like practicing any more than he felt like walking across a hot desert. And he wasn't alone. Half of the guys on the team felt the same way.

"Well — don't just stand there!" yelled Steve Herrick from first base at Jack Davis, the batter. "Swing that club, will you?"

If anybody could get irritable, it was Steve.

Chris looked at Coach Tony Edson, a short, frail-looking man who Chris found hard to believe was a former semipro baseball player. He wore a baseball cap and sweatshirt, and *looked* like a coach, but he was far from acting like one. You would expect a coach to give the boys instructions once in awhile. How to change their batting stances if they weren't hitting well, for example. Or how to change their fielding habits if they weren't fielding well.

Not him. All he'd done so far was to say, "Scatter out on the field, boys. Two or three of you bat. Hit five and bunt. Lewis, get on the mound." And he hadn't said more than three or four words since.

Coach Edson never said much anyway, but Chris remembered that it was the coach who had helped him on his batting last year.

4

Chris used to stand too far from the plate and kept his bat on his shoulder. "Stand closer to the plate, Chris," Coach Edson had said. "And hold the bat a few inches off your shoulder. Don't just let it rest there."

Something was different about Coach Edson this year. He was quieter than he'd ever been.

Jack Davis finally got his hits, then bunted a pitch down the third-base line. He dropped the bat, pulled his glove out of his hip pocket, and ran out to cover shortstop.

Two boys headed for the plate at the same time, Tex Kinsetta and Spike Dunne.

"I was waiting longer than you," snorted Tex.

"So?" said Spike.

Coach Edson was sitting in the dugout, writing on a pad. He didn't seem to notice what was going on.

"Oh, knock it off, will you?" shouted Steve. "Let's get the show moving!"

Coach Edson looked up. "Stop arguing, boys," he said. "Bat, Tex."

Glumly, Spike moved back, and Tex stepped into the batting box. Chris looked at Steve and saw the tall, dark-haired youth turn and shake his head.

Steve Herrick was the oldest boy on the team and the best player, too. Time and time again his hitting and fielding had helped the Blazers win ball games last year. But it was really Coach Edson who had made the Blazers a well-knit team. It was he who had kept them from going into the dumps when they lost. It was he who had given wise counsel when they were in a tough spot. They couldn't possibly have done well without him.

Why was he so different now? What was

wrong? Was he ill? He looked healthy enough.

Tex took his cuts, then dropped his bat, got his glove, and ran out to third base. Chris decided that he'd better take his batting practice now too, before the coach called for infield practice.

He trotted off the field, tossed his glove aside, and went to the pile of bats. He picked out one he liked, slipped a metal "doughnut" over the handle to the fat part of the bat, and swung the club back and forth a few times over his shoulders. When he removed the weight, the bat felt like a feather.

Steve Herrick trotted in, too.

"What's up with Coach?" he asked quietly.

"I don't know," answered Chris.

"Maybe he's tired of coaching us."

"Maybe. But he'd say so, wouldn't he?"

"It seems so."

Chris watched the tall first baseman pick up a bat. "This will be your second time at bat, won't it?" he asked.

"Yeah. Why not — if he doesn't say anything?"

"Well, we should have infield practice, too. And outfield."

"He's the coach," grunted Steve, looking briefly in Coach Edson's direction. "Not me. And not you, either."

Chris caught the implication, but carried it no further. He didn't want to put a chip on Steve's shoulder, a thing too easy to do.

He waited for Spike to finish batting, then stepped to the plate.

"Wait a minute, Chris." Coach Edson's interruption was a surprise. "Abe Ryan! Come in and pitch! Bill, have you batted yet?"

"No, sir."

8

"Okay. Follow Steve. Then we'll have infield."

Chris exchanged a glance with Steve. "Guess he's alive, anyway," mumbled Steve.

Chris missed Abe Ryan's first two pitches, then dropped to the ground from a wild one the left-hander threw at his head. He got up, dusted himself off, adjusted his glasses, and faced Abe again.

The tall lefty wound up and grooved the next pitch. Chris, a right-handed batter, swung and fouled the ball to the backstop screen. He missed the next pitch and popped twice to the infield.

"Let 'im hit it, Abe!" cried Mick Antonelli from the outfield. "We haven't got all day!"

Abe tossed up the next pitch easily and Chris blasted it to deep left. A chuckle rippled from the infielders.

"Don't expect those fat balloons in a game, Chris!" laughed Steve.

9

Chris bunted the next slow pitch down to first base, ran to first, then gathered up his glove and trotted to his position at second.

After Steve and Bill Lewis batted, Coach Edson worked on the infielders. Tex Kinsetta had trouble fielding grounders at third base and began throwing his glove to the ground in disgust, as if he were blaming the mitt for his problem.

"You'll come around," said Coach Edson as he knocked out a grounder to the shortstop, Jack Davis.

Chris thought he'd say more than that. The coach might at least explain to Tex why he was missing the ball. But he didn't.

After infield practice the coach hit balls to the outfielders for fifteen minutes, then called in the team and announced practice again for tomorrow night.

"We definitely need a new coach," Steve said emphatically as he, Ken, Chris and Tex left the ball park. They had their baseball shoes strung over their shoulders and their gloves draped over their wrists. "I don't think we'll win any games with him as coach."

"But who's going to tell him that?" said Chris. "He's an old man. It'll break his heart."

"He looks as if it's half broken now," said Steve.

They reached the intersection where they had to split up. "So long," said Steve and crossed the street to his home, which was catercorner from the ball field. Living so close to the park was sure convenient. If Steve didn't want to go to the park to watch a ball game, he could watch it from his house.

Ken lived a block away; Chris and Tex

lived two blocks away and four houses apart.

Rock Center was a small town at the foot of the Smoky Mountains. It had no theaters and featured no big sporting events. So when baseball season opened, the stands were usually packed. Rock Center backed its Little Leaguers one hundred percent.

At quarter of seven that night Chris received a phone call from Tex Kinsetta. Tex had never sounded so excited in his life — not even when he had corked a grand slammer in last year's playoffs.

"You won't believe it, Chris!" he cried. "You just won't believe it!"

"Believe what, Tex?"

"This phone call I got! From some guy! He talked like a coach!"

"It wasn't Coach Edson?"

"Heck, no! I don't know who he was! He told me I wasn't playing my position at third base right!"

2

TEX KINSETTA came over early the
next morning.

"Hi, Mrs. Richards," he said, taking off
his baseball cap and grinning. "Is Chris up
yet?"

Chris heard Mom laugh. He was having
breakfast in the dining room and wasn't
surprised that Tex was here earlier than
usual. He probably hadn't slept a wink all
night, thinking about that phone call.

"Yes, he's up," said Mom. "He's having
breakfast. Have you had yours?"

"Oh, yes."

15

Chris leaned over and peered through the dining room doorway. "Hi, Tex."

Tex's real name was Sherman. The kids called him Tex because he hailed from Texas.

"Hi," he said.

"Tex got a phone call from some guy last night," he said to his mother. "He called to tell Tex what he wasn't doing right at third base."

"Oh?" Mom's eyebrows lifted. "Who was he?"

"He wouldn't tell me," replied Tex.

"That's funny," she said.

"Sure is," said Chris. He wiped his mouth, left the table and headed for the door. "We're just going outside, Mom."

"I rode my bike," said Tex. "Get yours and let's ride awhile."

As if the word "bike" was a signal, Chris's dog, Patches, began barking excitedly. He was tied to his house near the fence dividing the Richardses from their neighbors.

Chris grinned. "Okay if he comes along?"

"Why not?" said Tex. "He always does, doesn't he?" He laughed, and Chris went to unsnap the chain from Patches' collar. Patches, a small, lean dog chock-full of energy, leaped up and licked Chris's face, then followed Chris to the bike leaning against the garage wall.

"Wish I had his energy," said Tex. "Maybe I'd do better at third base."

"Get a collar and I'll chain you to Patches' house for a day," replied Chris.

They rode along the side of the street, turning carefully into the line of traffic only when a parked car was in their way. Patches trailed behind them like a faithful rear guard.

"I wonder how that guy knew you weren't playing your position right," said Chris. "I

17

didn't see anybody watching us practice yesterday, did you?"

"No. That's what gets me."

"What did he say?"

"He said I should bend my knees more on grounders and should hold my glove closer to my body instead of reaching out for the ball," replied Tex.

Chris looked at him. "Did his voice sound familiar to you?"

"Not a bit. Anyway, he didn't talk long. He probably realized I was nervous talking with a stranger, because I didn't do more than mumble a couple of times."

"He give his name?"

"No. I mentioned it to my father. He said if the guy calls again to hang up unless he gives his name."

"I wonder if he called any of the other guys, too," said Chris.

"Maybe. But how would he know who they were? That's what gets me."

"Yeah. Gets me, too," admitted Chris.

They rode to Chris's father's gas station, and told him about the call. He was under a car on the lift, giving it a lubrication job.

"You're sure there was no one sitting under a tree in the outfield?" he asked. He was a tall, strapping man with oil smudges on his face. "Somebody had to be watching you fellows practice."

Chris thought hard, but couldn't remember seeing anybody sitting or standing in the outfield. "Could be," he said. "But I'm sure there was nobody out there, Dad."

"Well, you've probably heard the last of it, anyway," said Dad.

The boys returned home and started to play pitch and catch, and to talk about the phone call, when Steve Herrick and Ken

Lane came around the corner of the house. The sight of them started Chris's heart pounding.

"Just throwing won't help you on ground balls, Richards," said Steve. "I don't think hitting you grounders would help, either."

Then he laughed and headed for Chris's bike, parked against the garage. He pulled it away, got on it, and rode it out of the driveway.

"Hey! What do you think you're doing?" cried Chris.

"Cool it," grunted Steve. "I'm not going to steal it."

He rode out, pumping hard. Just then Patches began barking furiously. Ordinarily Chris would have yelled "Patches," but he didn't, and the little animal hightailed after Steve.

The three boys ran to the driveway, paused, and a soft "Oh-oh" broke from Ken.

Patches had caught up with Steve and had sunk his teeth into Steve's right pantleg, deep enough to tear a long piece out of it.

Chris felt a mixture of worry and pride. He had been sure that Steve wouldn't have gotten away with riding the bike — not with Patches around. But he might've prevented the dog from ripping Steve's pants. He just hadn't tried.

Steve returned with the bike, slower than he had departed with it, and grunted sourly, "I'll get 'im for this. Just wait."

3

IT WAS almost noon when the telephone rang. Chris's mother turned down the flame under the toasted cheese sandwich she was preparing, and went to answer it.

Chris, sitting at the kitchen table, flipped the pages of a sports magazine and listened to Mom's end of the conversation. It was short.

"Okay, dear," she said. "He's here." She held the receiver out to Chris. "It's Dad," she said.

He took the phone. "Hi, Dad."

"Chris, Mr. Herrick just called. Said that

your dog ripped his son's pants. What's your story?"

"Tex and I were playing pitch and catch when Steve and Ken Lane came over," explained Chris. "Then Steve got on my bike, took off with it, and Patches took off after him."

"Oh. So Steve took off with your bike. Mr. Herrick didn't tell me that."

"Probably Steve didn't tell him," said Chris.

"Probably not. Well, all right. Fortunately, Patches didn't bite Steve's leg. And Mr. Herrick said that we don't have to buy his son a new pair of pants, which I had said I'd do. He said his wife would repair them."

"Was he sore, Dad?"

"No. He seems like a real nice guy. He's an invalid and seldom gets out of the house, he told me. Well, good-bye. I just wanted to hear your side of the story. That's all."

" 'Bye, Dad."

Later that afternoon Tex came to the house and he and Chris walked to the baseball park. Batting practice was already in session.

"Cover second awhile, then bat after Mick," said Steve Herrick from his position at first base. Bill Lewis was throwing in the pitches.

Chris frowned. "Where's Coach Edson?"

"He can't be here. He asked me to take over."

Tex stared at him. "For the season?"

"Don't get shook," snapped Steve. "Just for today."

"Phew! You had me worried," replied Tex, sighing.

Chris smiled and trotted out to second

base. When it was Mick's turn to bat, he went in, too. After Mick batted, Chris took his turn. He fouled Bill's first steaming pitch, blasted the next one into foul territory in right field, and hit the next two in the same place.

"Let up, Bill!" yelled Steve. "He can't get his bat around fast enough!"

Chris tightened his lips. Steve had hit the problem right on the head. *But what can I do about it?* he thought. *The pitches are strikes.*

He fouled three attempted bunts before Steve yelled to him to quit trying and let someone else bat. Hiding his disgust, he tossed aside his bat, picked up his glove, and ran out to second base.

After batting practice Ken Lane hit grounders to the infielders. His first hit to Chris, a fast, buzzing grounder, was to the second baseman's right side. Chris lunged for it and tried to backhand the hop, but didn't get within a foot of it.

Ken hit another, this time directly at him. Chris caught it easily, snapped it to Steve, and Steve fired it home.

The next time around, Ken again hit to Chris's right side, and again Chris failed to snare the hop.

"Knock 'em to him nice and easy, Ken," chided Steve.

Chris blushed. Ken, a friend of Steve's, was the Blazers' infield substitute. *I wonder if he's working on my weakness so that he can ease me out of the starting lineup,* thought Chris.

He wasn't surprised when, at last, Steve yelled, "Okay, Chris! Let Ken take your place for a while and you hit 'em!"

By the time practice ended, Chris was exhausted. He went home, showered, got into fresh clothes, and took Patches with him to Dutchmen's Creek.

He sat under a shady tree and watched the fish swim in the clear water. Later, he lay back and wrestled with Patches, his happy laughter mixing with the dog's low, steady growl.

Suddenly Patches bounced back and froze. His eyes looked up and beyond Chris. The growl started again. This time it had a definitely strong, angry sound to it.

Chris turned and saw Steve Herrick and Frank Bellows standing not ten feet away. And breaking loose from Frank's grasp was his German shepherd, Starky. The big dog bolted for Patches.

"Starky!" yelled Frank. "Get back here! Get back!"

But Starky paid no attention.

4

STARKY and Patches met head on. The bigger dog was twice the size of the smaller one, but size apparently meant nothing to Patches. He nipped at Starky, tangled with him, fought desperately, and seemed to be holding his own.

But even so Chris was afraid for him. The brave little animal couldn't possibly continue like this for long.

"No, Patches!" he yelled. "No more fighting!"

Frank rushed forward and grabbed

29

Starky's leash. "I'm sorry, Chris," he apologized. "He broke away from me."

Chris rushed forward too and picked Patches up in his arms. Then Frank looked at Steve and anger flashed in his eyes. "No wonder you wanted me to bring Starky. You wanted him to get in a fight with Patches."

Steve stood staring at the ground, his face red, his lips pressed firmly together.

"Why?" cried Frank. "Why did you want them to fight?"

Steve turned away, not answering.

"Patches ripped his pants when Steve took off on my bike yesterday," explained Chris. "He wanted to get even."

"Oh, man," said Frank. "No wonder he wouldn't tell me. He just said let's go for a walk to the creek and bring Starky along. He knew Starky doesn't get along with most other dogs."

They watched Steve walking away, his hands in his pockets.

"It was partly my fault," confessed Chris. "I could've stopped Patches if I'd yelled at him. I just let him go."

He felt Patches' heart beating hard as he held the little animal close to him. The dog's body felt hot. "Wonder if Coach Edson will be at practice tomorrow," he said, changing the subject.

"I don't know. Steve said that we have a scrimmage game with the Pipers. I hope Coach Edson will be there. I'm not crazy about playing under Herrick."

"Neither am I," admitted Chris.

When he got home he found that Mom had packed a picnic lunch. When Dad came home and washed up, the four of them (Patches was included), went to Rock Center Park and had their supper. Then they all went swimming and didn't get home till after nine o'clock.

Chris was glad to see Coach Edson at the scrimmage game the next day, Friday. But the coach was as quiet as he had been at the practice sessions, and Chris wondered how long it would be before he'd quit coming altogether.

The coach selected Steve as captain. A man who had come to watch the game agreed to act as umpire and flipped a coin to see which team would bat first. The Pipers' captain won the toss and chose to bat last.

The teams went through their usual warm-ups. Then the Pipers ran out to the field, and Tex Kinsetta, the Blazers' leadoff hitter, stepped to the plate.

Harvey Keller, the Pipers' tall right-hander, breezed in his pitches with ease and ran the count to three balls and one strike.

Then Tex socked a long ball to center, which the fielder nabbed for an easy out.

Wally Munson grounded out on the first pitch, and Steve Herrick belted a pitch through short for a neat single. Steve had been avoiding Chris, as if he were ashamed of yesterday's incident.

Mick Antonelli, the powerhouse, came up. He tugged at his sleeves and dug his toes into the dirt, then popped up to the pitcher.

Bill Lewis, pitching for the Blazers, seemed frightened when the first two Pipers hit safely. Then a strikeout and two grounders hit to the infield pulled him through.

Spike Dunne, leading off in the top of the second inning, struck out, bringing up Chris. Chris was about to swing at Harvey's first pitch, then decided against it. Strike one.

Harvey couldn't find the plate after that, and Chris walked. He perished on first, though, as Jack Davis flied out to left, and Frank Bellows grounded out to third.

The Pipers' leadoff man blasted a hit through second base, just a bit to Chris's right side, which he missed by inches. The hit turned into the Pipers' first run.

"Just can't field the balls hit on your right side, can you, Richards?" said Steve. His words felt like needle jabs. "You know what I'd do if I were coach, don't you?"

He didn't say what he'd do, but Chris knew. He'd play Ken Lane at second, that's what.

Bill Lewis led off in the top of the third, and Harvey Keller again had difficulty getting a pitch over the plate. Bill walked.

"Lay it down," the coach advised Tex.

Tex bunted the first pitch towards third, and Bill galloped to second safely. Tex was thrown out by four steps. Wally Munson

34

tied his shoelaces before stepping into the batting box, then cracked a double, scoring Bill. The Blazers' bench went wild.

Steve stepped cockily to the plate, swung as hard as he could on two pitches, missed them both, and fell on his rear after the second one.

Nice show, thought Chris. *Steve was always swinging for the fence.*

He corked the third pitch almost a half-mile into the sky. It paused, came down, and the third baseman caught it easily.

Steve returned to the dugout, ignoring the snide remarks from the fans.

Mick Antonelli took the "doughnut" off the fat part of his bat and walked up to the plate.

"Drive me in, Mick!" Wally yelled from second base.

Mick dropped to the dirt on Harvey's first pitch, dusted himself off, and faced

36

Harvey again. He looked determined not to let a good pitch go by him.

And none did. Harvey's next pitch, a chest-high fast ball, was met by Mick's bat with a resounding whack and went singing over the shortstop's head for a cool single. Wally scored, running well ahead of the ball the left fielder pegged in.

Spike flied out, ending the top of the third inning.

"Let's hold 'em, Bill!" yelled Chris.

The Piper leadoff drove a hot liner directly at Chris. It was like a rifle shot. Chris lifted his glove and boom! he had it.

"Look what I've got!" cried Steve Herrick.

Chris saw the grin on Steve's face and grinned back. He had to force it; he couldn't let Steve get under his skin all the time. Nothing would please the guy more.

Two successive pop-ups quickly ended the Pipers' half of the inning.

37

In the top of the fourth Chris belted a single through short, then scored on Jack Davis's triple to deep center field, putting the Blazers in the lead, 3 to 1. He headed for the dugout and plunked himself down beside the coach.

"We missed you yesterday, Coach," he said, not able to keep silent any longer. "Didn't you feel well?"

"No. And I don't feel great now, either." Coach Edson paused and began rubbing the thumbnail of his left hand. "I don't know, Chris. I may have to give up coaching. But I can't just quit. I can't let you guys down like that. No, sir. I'm not *that* sick."

"Can't you get somebody to help you till you're better?" asked Chris.

"Who? I should have an assistant, but I can't find one. Everybody seems to be too busy with his own work to give me any help."

Chris shook his head in sympathy for the coach, then turned his attention back to the game. Frank Bellows and Bill Lewis both grounded out. Tex singled, driving Davis home, and Wally struck out, ending the half-inning.

The Pipers came to bat and really broke loose. The first batter hit a sizzling grounder through Chris's legs that drew a groan from the Blazers' fans. It also drew a snide remark from Steve Herrick.

"Coach, when are you going to put Lane in there?" he yelled.

The coach seemed not to have heard, but he must have.

The second batter hit a slow grounder to short, which Jack Davis caught and pegged to second in an attempt for a double play. Chris missed the throw, drawing another yell from the fans — and from Steve.

The next Piper cracked a hot grounder to

second, which, this time, Chris caught. He pegged it home. Too high! A run scored, and the other two runners were safe on third and second.

Successive hits brought in three more runs. When the wild bottom half of the inning was over, the Pipers were leading, 5 to 4, and Chris wished he had never seen a baseball.

5

STEVE HERRICK was first man up in the top of the fifth. He was chewing gum like crazy as he stood in the box, facing Harvey Keller.

Keller wound up, delivered, and heaved a pitch so wild that not even the catcher could reach it.

"Ball!" boomed the ump.

The Pipers' catcher trotted to the back-stop screen, retrieved the ball, and pegged it to Keller. Keller's next pitch cut the inside corner for a strike.

His third pitch was about to groove the

plate when Steve swung. *Crack!* The ball sailed out to deep left field and dropped over the fence for a home run. The Blazers' bench whooped and hollered as Steve ran with long, easy strides around the bases.

"Nice hit, Steve," said Coach Edson softly.

Steve touched hands with those extended to him, but he never looked up. *Boy!* thought Chris. *What a peacock!*

Cleanup hitter Mick Antonelli tried to duplicate Steve's clout but succeeded only in hitting the ball to the center fielder. Don Mitchell, batting for Spike Dunne, struck out.

Chris, up next, wished that Coach Edson would suggest what to do. Hit away? Wait out the pitches? But the coach was silent, leaving the decision up to him. Chris decided to "wait 'em out."

The strategy worked. He walked.

The coach then had Ken Lane bat for

Jack Davis. Chris looked at Steve for his reaction and saw the tall, dark-haired boy looking directly at him. It was obvious what Steve was thinking. Why not substitute Ken for Chris? What was Chris doing that he should be kept in there?

I'm hitting the ball, that's what, thought Chris. *But I wouldn't expect Steve to consider that.*

Ken seemed nervous at the plate and whiffed on three straight pitches. Three outs.

"Wonder why he had Ken bat for Jack?" said a disgruntled-sounding voice behind Chris as he trotted out to the infield.

Chris looked around at Steve. "He wants to give every guy a chance, that's why."

"I know," said Steve. "But why Jack and not you? That's what I'd like to know."

Chris blushed. "Mr. Edson is still coach, Herrick. Not you."

Their eyes caught and held for a moment. Then Steve looked away and ran to his spot at first base. Chris grinned to himself. It was seldom that he had the last word with Steve.

The Pipers' leadoff man fouled the first two pitches, then let the next three go by him. All were balls. He then hit the three-two pitch directly at Chris. The ball was a soft, high-hopping grounder. Chris ran in to the edge of the grass, fielded the hop, pivoted on his right foot, and pegged to first.

A low throw! "Stretch!" yelled Chris. Instead, Steve waited for the ball to bounce to him. He missed it, and the hitter was safe.

"Throw 'em up, will you?" yelled Steve angrily.

"You should've stretched!" replied Chris.

"Oh, sure!"

Chris turned and kicked the dirt at his

feet. He had to agree partly with Steve. The throw was poor but it wasn't that bad. If Steve had stretched, he could have caught the ball.

A double sent the runner around to third, putting the Pipers in excellent position to break the 5–5 tie.

A hard, grass-cutting drive to Chris! He hardly had time to think about it as he reached for the hop, glanced at the runner on third, then whipped the ball on a bead to first. This time the throw was perfect. One out.

"Nice play, Chris!" cried Tex Kinsetta from third. *Sometimes,* thought Chris as he pushed his glasses up on his nose, *I have the feeling that Tex is the only friend I have.*

The next hit was a hard blow to short. It was in the air and Ken caught it without moving a step. Two outs.

"He's your man, Bill!" cried catcher Frank Bellows as another Piper stepped to the plate.

"Strike!" yelled the ump as Bill grooved the first pitch.

He delivered his second almost in the same spot. This time the batter swung. *Crack!* A devastating blow to right center! One run scored and then another. The hit was a three-bagger. And that was it for the Pipers as Bill fanned the next hitter.

Frank led off in the top of the sixth, the last inning. Keller walked him. Bill bunted the first pitch down the first base line, advancing Frank to second, and Chris frowned disgustedly. The coach hadn't signaled Bill to bunt.

Why did he take it onto himself to do it? Even though the coach hadn't advised the boys what to do more than two or three

46

times during the game, that still didn't give Bill the right to bunt on his own.

Then Chris remembered that he had waited out Keller's pitches when he had batted. Had he been right in doing so? He felt that that situation was different, though. He wasn't sacrificing himself as Bill had done.

Oh, man, they needed a good coach, all right. Needed one badly!

Tex took a strike, then lambasted a pitch to center. It was caught for out two. Wally Munson hit the first pitch to short and was thrown out by a step. The game was over. Pipers 7, Blazers 5.

"You and old buddy Herrick exchange a few words?" smiled Tex as he and Chris walked off the field together.

"A few," admitted Chris. "He thinks Ken should've taken my place instead of Jack's."

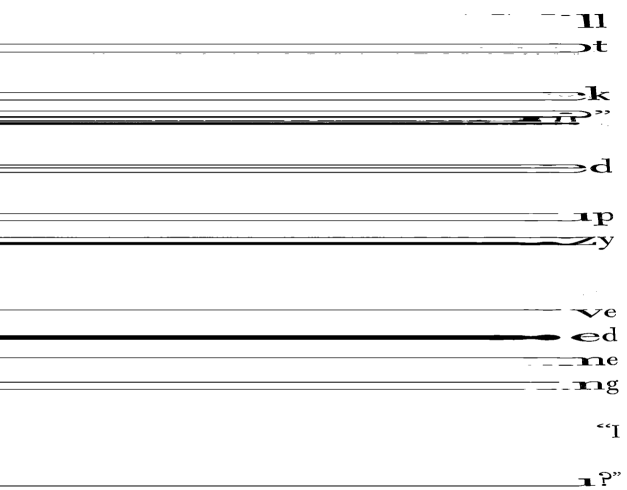

"Me?"

know."

He felt

really be

a man wHA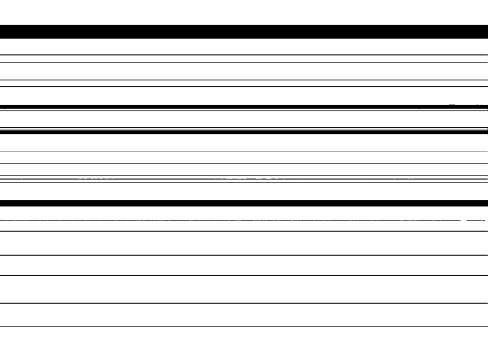

to call hi

plain you

more than

Then, a

was exactl

"Just w

on how you

base, Chri

"Do you m

"Who

heart pou

"Just ca

reply.

"So what? Maybe the next time Coach'll have Ken take your place. We've only got one sub infielder."

They reached Florida Avenue. "Did Mick tell you about his phone call last night?" asked Tex.

Chris stared at him. "That guy called him, too?"

Tex nodded. "Except that Mick hung up on him. He thought it was one of those crazy calls."

"What did the man say?"

"He started to tell Mick how to improve on his outfield position. When Mick asked him who he was, he just said 'Call me Coach,' as he'd said to me, and Mick hung up."

"Isn't that something?" said Chris. "I wonder who he is."

"What would you do if he called you?" asked Tex.

"Me?" Chris thought a moment. "I don't know."

He felt a shiver run up his spine. It must really be something to receive a call from a man who wouldn't tell his name except to call him Coach, and to listen to him explain your mistakes playing baseball. It was more than something. It was weird.

Then, at seven-thirty that evening, that was exactly what happened.

"Just want to offer a couple of suggestions on how you can improve yourself at second base, Chris," said the mild, pleasant voice. "Do you mind?"

"Who — who is this?" asked Chris, his heart pounding.

"Just call me Coach," came the gentle reply.

6

WELL . . . I . . . I don't know," answered Chris, his hand tightening on the receiver. "If you don't tell me who you are . . ."

"Well, I know how you feel about an anonymous call, Chris," the voice broke in. "But this isn't a call to scare you. I happen to be a baseball bug and all I'd like to do is offer you some pointers on how to improve your fielding skill, something your coach should be telling you, but isn't. If you don't want to listen, okay. I'll hang up."

The line was silent as Chris pondered

what to say. The man's intention seemed sound and honest. Tex had said, too, that the only thing the man had talked about was his mistakes. And every bit of it had made sense.

"Well . . . okay," agreed Chris.

"Thanks. Chris, you're always playing in the same spot whether a left-handed hitter or a right-handed hitter is batting. Play about halfway between first and second base and deeper on a left-handed hitter. On a right-handed hitter play closer to second base. You'll find that you'll be catching a lot of balls that have been going for hits."

Chris listened attentively, realizing that there was a lot of sense in that.

"One other thing for now, Chris. Bend your knees on low, sizzling grounders and get your glove down close to the ground. There you are, Chris. Work on those two pointers. You'll not only be a better ball-

52

player, but the teams you're playing against won't be scoring so much, either."

"Thanks, sir."

"Good night."

"Good night, Mr. . . ." He heard the phone click on the other end and remembered that he didn't know the man's name.

"Who was that?" asked Dad. He was standing in the doorway, holding a newspaper.

"I don't know," said Chris. "He wouldn't tell me his name."

"Oh?" Dad frowned. "A stranger?"

Chris looked at his father. "You and Mom warned me against talking to strangers, Dad, even over the telephone. But this was different."

"In what way?"

"He suggested how I could play my position better at second base. He told me what I was doing wrong and how to correct it."

Chris's eyes lit up. "That's exactly what we need, Dad! Advice! Coach Edson hardly ever opens his mouth."

"Hmmm," murmured Dad. "Well . . . seems to be no harm in that. Did he say why he wouldn't tell his name?"

"No. And I'm not the only guy he's talked to so far, Dad. He's also talked to Tex and Mick. Tex listened to him, but Mick didn't."

"Why not?"

"You know Mick. Nobody can tell him anything . . . especially a guy who wouldn't give his name."

"Hmmm," Dad murmured again. "It seems that the man, whoever he is, has taken an interest in your team, all right. And he seems to know baseball, too. Have you seen any strangers at the ball park?"

"No. That's what Tex and I can't figure out. Who could know so much about us without being at our practices or at the game?"

Amusement flashed in Dad's eyes. "Seems that your telephone friend not only likes baseball, but likes to play the mystery man, too. Well . . ." he rustled the paper as he turned to go back into the other room, "as long as he's trying to help you boys play better baseball, I see no harm in his telephoning."

"Why do you think he doesn't want his identity known, Dad?"

His father shrugged. "I don't know. Maybe he doesn't want Mr. Edson to know."

"Because Mr. Edson might get sore?"

"Could be."

Chris dialed Tex's number, got Tex after a couple of rings and told him about the call. Tex expressed surprise, then wanted to know what the man said. Chris told him, adding that the man seemed to be an expert on baseball, but that it was sure funny he wouldn't tell his name.

"Maybe he figures nobody knows him, anyway," ventured Tex.

"Could be," said Chris. "I tried to recognize his voice, but I couldn't. I don't think I ever heard it before."

"Me neither," admitted Tex. "It's sure spooky, isn't it?"

"Well, sort of weird," agreed Chris.

There was a long silence, then Tex asked, "You all set for our first league game?"

"When is it?"

"Thursday. Against the Scorpions. Maybe our mystery coach will be there."

"How will we know him?"

"Just yell 'Coach!' and see which guy raises his hand," said Tex, laughing.

"Clown," muttered Chris.

At ten o'clock the next morning Tex was at the house with two other members of the Blazers, Jack Davis and Don Mitchell. If Tex looked excited, Jack and Don looked even more so.

"You know what?" cried Tex before Chris had the door completely open. "These guys got telephone calls, too!"

Chris stared. "From 'Coach'?"

"Who else?"

7

THE BOYS started some detective work to pin down the identity of the man who called himself "Coach."

"I know it's not *my* father," said Chris. "It would be ridiculous for him to call me. Besides, I'd recognize his voice. How about you, Tex? Was your father home when the man called you?"

"Yes. But if the man's the father of one of our players, then that player would know, wouldn't he?"

"Okay," said Steve Herrick. "Let's settle

it now. Whose father is making the phone calls?"

"Not mine," some of them answered. Others shook their heads.

"Man!" said Mick. "If it's not one of our fathers, who is it?"

"Somebody who's interested in us, that's for sure," replied Chris.

The opening day of the baseball season came around and the Scorpions had first raps. The July sun was hot, and Chris had already worked up a sweat from infield practice.

A nice crowd filled the stands. Chris knew that somewhere among the many faces were Mom and Dad.

Abe Ryan, the Blazers' tall, dark-haired left-hander, got his signal from catcher Frank Bellows, stretched, and delivered. The ball grooved the center of the plate for a strike.

Frank returned the ball to Abe, and the lefty went into his motions again.

"Strike two!" yelled the ump as the ball cut the inside corner.

"Nice pitch, Abe, ol' boy!" yelled Chris Richards, socking the pocket of his glove with his fist. "Strike 'im out!"

The other infielders joined in the line of chatter.

Wham! The Scorpion drove Abe's third pitch over second for a clean hit.

Tex and Steve played in closer, anticipating a bunt, but the move didn't discourage the Scorpion batter. He laid a beauty on the ground between third base and the mound, which Abe Ryan went after, scooped up, and rifled to first.

"Out!" yelled the base umpire, thumb jabbing the air. The runner advanced safely to second.

The next Scorpion popped a high fly to

second base that Chris yelled for and caught. Two outs.

Chris remembered the mystery coach's advice to play closer to second base on a right-handed hitter, and deeper and halfway between first and second on a left-handed hitter. It sure made sense.

Then — a shot on a straight line to Tex at third base. He caught it with a quick move of his glove, stared at the ball as if he were surprised he had it, then tossed it toward the mound and trotted in to the Blazers' bench.

"Surprised you had it?" Chris chuckled.

Tex laughed. "Know what? I was!"

The fans cheered the Texan as he stepped to the plate. He fouled off three pitches, took a ball, then flied out to center. Wally, whose mass of red hair made his protective helmet sit high on his head, belted the first pitch for a single. A born showman, Wally bowed to the cheering fans.

"Look at him," said Tex. "Thinks he's a Hollywood star."

Steve Herrick went through his regular motions of putting both hands in the dirt, rubbing them off, and swinging the bat over his head a few times before stepping into the box. All this went for nothing as he socked a grounder to third base. The Scorpion caught the hop, glanced at second, then heaved the ball to first to throw Steve out.

Mick, the Blazers' cleanup hitter, drove a long ball to deep left for a triple, scoring Wally. Spike Dunne walked and it looked as if the Blazers were really having a hot inning. But Chris, on the two-two pitch, swung at a high one and struck out.

"If you like pitches over your head," said Steve as he ran out to the field with Chris, "why don't you use a flagpole? You might be able to reach 'em."

"Very funny," said Chris.

Abe Ryan lost control of his first pitch and hit the Scorpion leadoff man on his hip. The Scorpion dropped his bat and trotted to first base.

"Let's get two!" yelled Chris. He moved closer to second base as a right-handed batter stepped into the box.

Crack! A hot grounder to short. Jack fielded it, whipped it to Chris and Chris pegged it to first. A double play!

A high pop-up to Frank Bellows ended the top half of the second inning.

"He's got nothing on it," Steve Herrick said to Jack, referring to Howie Little, the Scorpions' pitcher. "It's as straight as a string."

Jack corked Howie's second pitch through the second baseman's legs, then advanced to third on Frank's double to left center field. Abe, batting left-handed, drilled one out to deep right. The ball was caught, but Jack tagged up, then scored.

Tex knocked Frank in on a single over short, then perished on base when both Wally and Steve flied out.

Scorpions 0, Blazers 3.

The Blazers were hot.

The Scorpions' leadoff man tagged Abe's first pitch for a triple, then scored on a two-bagger to deep right field. Chris looked at Abe, hoping that the two long hits wouldn't make him so nervous that he'd lose control and start walking every Scorpion coming to bat.

But that was exactly what was starting to happen. Abe walked the next two Scorpions to fill the bases.

"Take your time, Abe!" Chris shouted. "Groove 'em!"

He felt the tension beginning to grow

among the Blazers. A long hit could wipe the bases clean and put the Scorpions ahead.

"Ball!" shouted the ump as Abe breezed in his first pitch.

A strike followed. Then three consecutive pitches, none of which crossed the plate, sent the batter to first and walked in the Scorpions' second run.

Chris stared across the diamond at Coach Edson. *Coach! Aren't you going to do something? Can't you see that Abe's completely lost control of his pitches?*

A hard drive to third! A ball that sailed through the air like a rocket. Tex intercepted it. One out. He touched third — two outs. He rifled the ball to first. Three outs!

A triple play!

The Blazer fans went wild and cheered Tex as he ran in to the bench.

"Thanks, Tex," murmured Abe, relief bright on his face. "You saved my life."

Tex laughed. "Anytime, Abe," he said.

Mick Antonelli led off in the bottom of the third and dropped a single behind first base. He'd hit the ball at the end of his bat. Spike Dunne tagged a long one to left but it wasn't long enough. The ball was caught and pegged to second to hold Mike on first. One out.

Chris stepped into the box, anxious to redeem himself after that strikeout in the first inning. He let the first pitch go by — a called strike — then dropped to the dirt on a close throw.

He got up, dusted himself off, then belted a waist-high pitch to left center field. The blow was high and it looked for a moment as if it might drop over the fence. It didn't. It struck the fence, bounced back, and the fielder picked it up and pegged it in. The shortstop caught it and relayed it to third in an attempt to get Chris. The throw was late and Chris was on for a triple with an RBI credited to him.

There, Mr. Herrick, he thought, looking at Steve. *How do you like those sour apples?* But Steve wasn't looking at him.

Jack Davis popped up to the catcher and Frank grounded out to short, ending the half-inning.

Scorpions 2, Blazers 4.

The Scorpions came up in the top of the fourth as if their stingers had all been plucked. Chris felt sure that this would be the fastest half-inning ever.

He was wrong.

The first Scorpion drilled Abe's first pitch through the mound, almost knocking Abe's pins from under him. The next cracked a double to right center, advancing the runner to third.

Abe stood off the mound awhile, wiped his sweating forehead, then stepped back on

the rubber. He checked the runners on second and third, then delivered. *Smack!* A hard grounder between Chris and second base! Chris sprang for it, but the ball brushed the tip of his glove and bounded to the outfield. He landed on his belly, mad at himself for having forgotten to play his position where he should have on the right-handed hitter. He had been playing it as if a left-hander were batting.

Two runs scored.

The next hit was a soft fly behind second. Chris, still hurt thinking about the previous play, dropped back.

He reached for the ball — and missed it! The runner on first bolted for second and the hitter was safe.

"Richards!" bawled Steve Herrick angrily. "What do you need to catch a ball? A basket?"

8

CHRIS KICKED at the dirt, wishing he could make himself invisible. He was playing the worst he had ever played. Steve was right. He should use a basket instead of a glove.

"Forget it, Chris!" Tex yelled from third. "Get the next one!"

Oh, sure, thought Chris. *But the next one won't cancel out the error I made on that easy, blooping fly.*

Abe Ryan managed to put two strikes over the plate on the next Scorpion, then was hit for a single that brought in another run. A pop-up to Tex and then a slow grounder to short accounted for two quick outs. Now the runners were on second and third and the Scorpions' cleanup hitter was at the plate.

Abe pitched to him. His first two throws were so wide that Frank had to stretch for them. His next pitch cut the inside corner for a strike. Then the Scorpion lambasted a belt-high pitch to left center field for a double, and both runners scored.

"Time!" yelled Steve Herrick.

"Time!" echoed the umpire.

Steve trotted toward the mound, looking at Coach Edson sitting in the dugout. Chris looked too. You'd think that the coach had his mind a thousand miles away. But suddenly he turned to Bill Lewis sitting beside him and motioned him to go in.

Bill dragged himself out of the dugout and to the mound as if he were loaded down with weights.

What a team, thought Chris. Bill should have been warming up ever since the Scorpions had started to knock Abe's pitches all over the lot. But it was Coach Edson's job to have instructed Bill to do so. No one else's.

A smattering of applause rose as Abe Ryan walked off the field, his head bowed. He handed the ball to Bill, who stepped to the mound and started to do what he should have been doing in the bull pen.

After seven or eight throws the umpire called time-in and the game resumed.

Bill hurled his first pitch too far inside. The hitter couldn't dodge it and was hit.

"Take your base!" cried the ump.

This is just great, fumed Chris. *From the frying pan into the fire.*

The next Scorpion went the limit, then

smacked the three-two pitch for a high-hopping grounder to second. The ball was to Chris's right side, but he was playing his position as the mystery coach had reminded him to do on a right-handed hitter. He caught the ball, made the play at second base unassisted, and the terrible half-inning was over.

He headed for the drinking fountain behind the dugout.

"Well, where are you going on your vacation?" asked a voice behind him.

He turned, spat out part of the water, and frowned at Steve Herrick. "What vacation?"

"What vacation? The Blazers have fallen apart, man! Didn't you see what went on out there? You were a part of it."

"I'm no pro," said Chris. "Neither is anybody else."

Mick Antonelli came running forward. "Man, did we blow that lead," he exclaimed.

"And Bill wasn't even warmed up when he went to the mound!"

Chris's temper flared as he looked from Mick to Steve. "What do you mean? That this is it? That we won't be playing other games just because the Scorpions had a hot time at bat?"

"At the same time you and some other guys played like real beginners," said Steve, matching Chris's tone of voice.

"Besides that, Coach Edson just sits in the dugout like a statue," added Mark. "I'm with Steve. I think we ought to fold."

"You don't want to give us a chance!" retorted Chris. "This is only our first game!"

"Our second," corrected Steve. "We lost one the other day."

"That was a practice game!"

"So is this as far as I'm concerned," replied Mick, and started to walk toward the dugout.

Steve caught up with him. Chris trailed, still seething.

"If you quit," he said, "you're a couple of cowards."

Both turned. "Listen," snorted Steve. "You want to see us lose every game? You want everybody in the neighborhood to laugh at us everytime they see us? Is that what you want?"

"How do you know we'll lose every game? Sure we will if we don't stick together. But we've got to stick together."

"Then we'll have to get rid of Coach Edson and get a new coach," said Mick.

"Who's going to tell him that?" asked Chris, eyeing Mick unflinchingly. "Are you?"

"No. But somebody should."

"Sure. And break his heart," said Chris. "Make him sicker than he already is."

"Come on," said Steve. "If I'm lucky, I'll be up this inning."

They reached the front of the dugout and saw that Bill Lewis was on first base.

"How'd he get on?" asked Steve.

"Singled over short," replied Spike.

Tex Kinsetta was batting. He had two strikes on him, then belted the next pitch to the pitcher. The Scorpion snared the hop and whipped it to second for the first out. The second baseman pegged to first to complete a quick double play.

"Save me a rap, Don!" cried Steve.

Don Mitchell, pinch-hitting for Wally Munson, did. He cracked a single over second. Then Steve drilled one through the hole between left and center for two bases. But the Scorpion center fielder, a fast man with an excellent throwing arm, kept Don from scoring.

Mick, batting next, flied out to third.

Scorpions 7, Blazers 4.

In the top of the fifth Don misjudged a fly

in left field, permitting the hitter to chalk up two bases on the error. The next Scorpion blasted a drive over Chris's head for a single, scoring a run, and Chris feared another wild half-inning. That would give both Steve and Mick more to chew on.

Two walks in a row filled the bases, and the next hitter was a left-handed batter.

Chris, his heart pounding, moved closer toward first base and waited.

9

CRACK! A sharp blow to second base! Chris caught the hop and pegged it home. Out!

Frank whipped the ball to first, but the hitter was there by two steps. There were still three men on.

"Get two!" shouted Chris.

Bill Lewis stepped to the mound. He looked at the runners, stretched, and delivered. A hard blow to short! Jack reached for the hop. The ball glanced off his glove, struck his chest, and rolled to the ground.

Quickly Jack retrieved it and snapped it to second. Chris, covering the bag, caught the ball for the out, and fired it to third.

"Safe!" yelled the ump.

Two outs. In the meantime another run had crossed the plate.

Chris ran out to his position and looked at Steve. The first baseman was standing at ease beside the bag, his arms crossed, his eyes hard as glass. It didn't take two guesses to know what was boiling in his mind.

The next Scorpion popped to Frank, ending the half-inning. The Scorpions now led, 9 to 4.

"Start it off, Spike," said Coach Edson.

Steve looked at him in surprise, then at Chris. *Hey! He's alive!* his expression seemed to say.

Spike cracked out a double and the Blazer fans cheered. "Keep it going, Blazers!" yelled a fan.

They didn't. Ken, pinch-hitting for Chris, grounded out, Jack fanned, and Frank hit an easy grounder to first.

The Scorpions managed to put two hits back to back at their turn at bat in the top of the sixth, resulting in another run. That was all, but it was plenty. The Blazers drew a goose egg and the game was over, the Scorpions winning it, 10 to 4.

"You still think we have a chance?" Steve asked bitterly as he walked off the field with Chris, Ken and Tex.

"Yes, I do," replied Chris. "I haven't changed my mind."

That evening the phone rang, and Chris jumped with a start from his chair. His first thought was that the caller was the mystery coach.

It was Tex and his voice was quivering with excitement.

"Chris! Spike Dunne just called me! He got a call from the coach, too!"

"The mystery coach?"

"Right!"

"What did he say?"

"He told Spike to move over about ten feet toward center field on a right-handed hitter and closer toward the right field foul line on a left-handed hitter. Apparently Spike always played in the same spot regardless of who batted."

Chris pondered a thought, then said, "Tex, do you think *he'd* coach us if we asked him?"

"That's an idea. But we don't know who he is, and who he's going to call next. How can we ask him?"

"I know," admitted Chris. "But that's only one problem. The other problem is Coach Edson himself. He's not doing the team any good, and we can't tell him to leave. If he's sick now he'll be sicker if we tell him how we feel."

"Maybe he'd get the hint if we picked up another coach," said Tex.

"Maybe he would. I don't know, Tex. I hate to agree with Herrick and Antonelli, but I'm afraid we are falling apart."

"Yeah. Me, too," said Tex sadly.

The second league game was against the Gators, a team considered the one to beat if the Blazers expected to stay in the league and climb to the top of the heap.

The chief worry now wasn't the Gators, however. It was Coach Edson. He might as well have stayed home rather than sit on the bench and just be a spectator. Even some of the spectators were offering more advice than he was.

But who, among the Blazers, would tell him to quit?

Chris glanced at the team members sitting with him on the bench. All of them seemed as empty of spirit as a deflated balloon was of air. And what put them in such a mood? Not having a coach who cared!

"Is the lineup the same as it was before, Coach Edson?" asked Steve Herrick, swinging a bat with a "doughnut" on it.

"No change," answered the coach quietly.

Tex Kinsetta led off. He went the full count, three-two, then walked. Mitch Rogers, the Gators' tall, red-headed pitcher, kicked the dirt in front of the rubber as if that were where his problem was, then got into position as Wally Munson came to bat.

Wally took a two-two count, then blasted a pitch to short center. The fly was caught and Tex trotted back to first.

Steve Herrick, in spite of drilling two foul balls over the fence, flied out to left for the second out. Mick Antonelli socked Mitch's first pitch through the hole between third and short for a single, then Spike Dunne walked, filling the bases.

Chris stepped to the plate, welcomed by a thunderous cry from the Blazer fans.

He took a called strike, then two balls. The next pitch was in there, and he swung. A pop-up to second base.

Disgusted, he tossed the bat aside and started to walk toward first. He watched the ball descend, the second baseman waiting for it. The ball struck the player's glove — then dropped to the ground!

In a flash Chris spurted for first base. At the same time the Gator second baseman picked up the ball, and fired it. The throw beat Chris by three steps.

"Out!" yelled the ump.

Chris, head bowed, walked back to the dugout, got his glove and ran out to his position at second. A fan yelled, "Always run 'em out, Chris!"

He hoped he'd never forget that advice.

The Gators got onto Abe Ryan's pitches for two hits and two runs to go into a quick lead, 2 to 0.

"It could've been two and two," said Steve as he ran in with Chris at the end of the first inning.

Chris looked at him but said nothing.

Jack Davis started off the second inning with a single over second on Mitch Rogers' first pitch. Frank Bellows flied out, then Abe Ryan singled through short, advancing Jack to second.

Tex was up next. Chris saw him glance at the coach for a sign, but the coach was sitting with his arms crossed over his chest, his head back against the dugout wall and his eyes, of all things, closed!

He's asleep! thought Chris disbelievingly. But, as he looked closer, he saw that the coach's eyes were really open.

Crack! A hard grounder to second. The Gator second baseman caught the hop, dropped it, picked it up, and shot it to first. Out!

Men on second and third, and Wally Munson came to bat. He belted a soft pitch over short, and Spike Dunne, coaching at third, windmilled Jack in. The throw-in from left field was late and Jack scored. Steve, swinging for the fence, flied out to left. Three outs.

Blazers 1, Gators 2.

The Gators' leadoff man drilled a pitch directly at Chris. The ball never climbed more than six feet and Chris nabbed it for the out. Abe mowed down the next Gator on strikes, then spoiled matters by hitting the next batter on the thigh.

A soft grounder to short, which the shortstop muffed, advanced the runner to second and scored a hit for the batter. That was the extent of it. The next Gator bounced a pitch back at Abe and Abe fired it to first for a fast out. Three outs.

Mick led off in the top of the third and flied out. Spike struck out, and Chris stepped to the plate, wondering if he was to be the third victim. He took a ball, then two strikes, then blasted a hit to deep left. He rounded first . . . second . . . and started for third. Steve, coaching there, waved him back.

Jack Davis grounded out, and that was it.

The Gators came to bat. The leadoff man, a lefty, bunted safely down to third, then advanced to second on a sacrifice bunt. Two consecutive hits put two runs across, and the Gators led, 4 to 1.

Frank Bellows, leading off for the Blazers, belted the first pitch for a long triple. Abe grounded out. Frank stayed on third, not daring to take the chance to run in.

Mitch Rogers wiped his face with the

back of his glove, then breezed in a low pitch to leadoff hitter Tex Kinsetta. *Smack!* A single through short, and Frank scored.

Wally fouled three pitches, then flied out to left, and up came Steve Herrick. He drilled a long foul to left, then uncorked the big one — a long home run over the left field fence.

"Thatta way to go, Steve!" yelled Ken Lane as Steve trotted around the bases.

Mick Antonelli kept up the rally with a single. But Don Mitchell, pinch-hitting for Spike, flied out and the big half-inning was over.

Blazers 4, Gators 4.

"Okay, guys!" cried Steve as the team ran out to the field. "Let's hold 'em!"

Hold 'em they did. But the Gators held the Blazers from scoring in the fifth too, and came to bat in the bottom of the inning with their big guns leading off. The bats of the big guns boomed to the tune of one run, putting them ahead, 5 to 4.

Tex beat out a scratch hit to short, but both Wally and Steve got out, leaving the Blazers a very slim chance of winning. Mick walked, and Don came up, anxiously swinging his bat at the first pitch. *Crack!* A long fly to center. It was caught and the game was over.

Blazers 4, Gators 5.

"That's three games in a row we've lost, Coach Edson," said Chris.

"The first was a practice game," countered the coach, popping the baseballs into a blue bag. "Don't worry. We'll get going."

"When?" asked Steve.

The coach looked at him. He zippered up the bag and rose to his feet. He was just a couple of inches taller than Steve.

"Steve, you think I don't know what you and the rest of the boys have been saying about me?"

Steve blushed. So did Chris. They looked at each other, then at the other boys standing nearby, then at the coach.

"I know," said the coach, "and I can't blame you. I know I'm not doing the job I should, but I can't help it. I haven't felt well, but I didn't want to quit coaching." He paused as he looked at the faces around him. "My doctor told me to take it easy. I guess I have been. Too easy."

A smile cracked Chris's face, and then Steve's.

"Get another coach if you can," suggested Coach Edson. "But it's not easy. I know. A lot of men were asked to coach before me. Perhaps things have changed in the last three years. I don't know. But try. Don't worry, I won't get sore. I'm all for it. I just didn't want you boys to play without a coach, that's all. It's my job. I promised you I'd do it, but I didn't know my health was going to go bad. That's something no one knows."

The boys looked at him solemnly.

"Git, now," he ordered. "You look sicker than I do. And don't worry. Losing another game won't stop the world."

10

THE PHONE rang at seven-thirty that
evening and Chris's heart jumped as
he ran to answer it.

"Hello?"

"Chris?"

Chris relaxed, disappointed. He had hoped
it would be the mystery coach.

"Hi, Wally."

"I just got a call from that guy you said
had been calling up you and Tex and other
guys on our team," said Wally nervously.

"What did he say?"

"He said that I should've bunted in the

first inning to get Tex on second base in position to score. I told him that Mr. Edson was our coach, and he didn't tell me to bunt or not to bunt, so I hit. He said he understood, and then he apologized."

"His idea makes sense," said Chris, recalling the situation. "Tex could've advanced to third on Steve's fly and scored on Mick's single. We would've had a run in that first inning."

The line was silent a moment, then Wally exclaimed, "Hey, that's right!"

Ten minutes later the phone rang again. This time it was Tex. He, too, had received a call from the mystery coach.

"He said I played too deep on that left-handed leadoff man in the third inning," said Tex. "If I had played in, the guy wouldn't have bunted. Remember? He got a hit out of it, then advanced to second on the next batter's sacrifice bunt."

"I remember," replied Chris. "That's all he told you?"

"Well . . . he said I was hitting pretty good."

Chris could picture Tex smiling proudly as he said that. "Good," he said, grinning. "See you, Tex."

He had hardly hung up when the phone rang again. He picked it up, thinking it was still another member of the Blazers. It wasn't. The sound of the soft, deep-throated voice made his heart pound.

"Chris? This is Coach again. Tough game to lose, wasn't it?"

"Yeah," said Chris, breathing hard. "It sure was. Did . . . did you see it?"

"Oh, I saw it, all right. And I know how you must've felt when you didn't run out that pop fly that the Gators' second baseman missed."

Chris nodded, admitting his laziness to

96

the unseen speaker. "I'll never let that happen again," he promised.

The mystery coach chuckled. "I'm sure that'll stick in your mind for a long time," he said. "By the way, that was a nice catch you made."

"Thanks, sir."

"Good night, Chris."

"Sir!"

"Yes, Chris?"

"Sir, Coach Edson isn't well. He's coming to our games only because he feels he's obligated to. But he's not telling us what to do, and we . . . we're lost, sir. He said he'd quit if we can get another coach." Chris paused and lifted his glasses slightly on his nose. "Would . . . would you coach us, sir?"

There was a long silence while Chris waited patiently for the mystery coach's answer.

Finally it came. "Thanks, Chris, but I can't. Good night."

The phone clicked on the other end and Chris hung up, his heart heavy. There, down the drain, went the best possibility for a coach.

He sat there a long while, thinking of the men he knew who could be available as coaches. There seemed to be a lot of them, but nearly all of them were already involved in other youth projects. Then he thought of Steve Herrick. Had Steve asked his father yet? He decided he'd call.

He looked up the Herricks' number in the directory, then dialed it.

"Hello?" said a woman's voice.

"Mrs. Herrick?"

"Yes."

"This is Chris Richards. Is Steve there?"

"Just a minute, please." There was a pause, then Steve's voice answered. "Hello?"

"Steve? This is Chris. Have you asked your father yet about coaching us?"

"No."

"You going to?"

"No, because I'm sure he won't. Is that all you want to ask me?"

"Yes."

"Okay. Good-bye," said Steve, and hung up.

11

TEX CAME to the house the next day on his bike, bringing along his swimming trunks. Chris got his and together they rode to Dutchmen's Creek. Patches, as usual, trailed along.

They had been swimming for almost half an hour when Ken Lane stopped by. Chris frowned. "Where's Steve?" he asked.

"He and his mother went to Knoxville," replied Ken. He dropped on the grass, broke off a blade and stuck it between his teeth. "Hear the news?"

The boys looked at him. "What news?"

"Coach Edson was taken to the hospital."

"Oh, no!" cried Chris. "What happened?"

"He has a kidney disease. His wife called my mother and told her."

"No wonder he wasn't well!" said Tex. "What're we going to do now? Fold up?"

Ken shrugged. "Might as well. We're just making chumps of ourselves, anyway."

Chris stared at him. "Is that what Steve says, too?"

"Sure. And I agree with him."

Chris looked at him awhile, and finally asked, "Ken, have you ever tried to think for yourself?"

Ken's face reddened. He yanked a handful of grass out of the ground and stared at Chris. "Steve and I are friends. We think alike. Okay?"

He got up, started to leave, and looked over his shoulder. "I didn't want to tell you this yet, but now I will. Besides a coach, you'll need a new infield sub and a guy to fill in the third spot in the Blazers' batting order. See ya."

With that he ran off, singing some rock tune.

"He's lying," said Chris, watching Ken vanish behind the trees. "He made up that lie on the spot."

"But what're we going to do about a coach, Chris?" Tex sounded worried. "Ken's right when he said we'd be making chumps of ourselves."

Chris shook his head. "I don't know what we're going to do, Tex," he said dismally.

The next morning they picked up the baseball equipment from Coach Edson's house, but when the game was supposed to start the following afternoon, Chris wasn't sure whether the Blazers would be able to field nine men. After that angry remark Ken had made to Chris at Dutchmen's Creek yesterday, it was just possible that both he and Steve wouldn't be at the park.

And they weren't. Every single Blazer was present except Steve Herrick and Ken Lane.

The rats, thought Chris. *The crummy rats. They had let Coach Edson down.*

Well, they still had enough men to field a team. But who was going to run it? Somebody had to.

"Chris, it looks like you'll have to be our captain," said Tex. "I've talked with the guys and they've agreed that you're the only one who can do it."

Chris looked at the faces around him. Long, sad faces. *They know we don't have a chance of winning,* he thought. *They're only here because of Coach Edson.*

And then Tex let out a wild yell. "Hey, Chris! Look!"

Chris looked, and so did everyone else. There, coming through the gate at the left of the grandstand, were Steve Herrick and Ken Lane — pushing a man in a wheelchair!

"Who's that?" Chris asked.

"I don't know!" Tex answered.

Steve and Ken pushed the man towards the dugout. A silence hung like a heavy veil as the man smiled and looked at the boys facing him. He was in his late fifties, gray-haired, and wore a white, short-sleeved shirt.

"Hello, boys," he said in a soft, moderate voice. "I'm Mr. Herrick, Steve's father."

Chris stared and exchanged a look with Tex. No wonder Steve hadn't wanted to ask his father to coach the team. He was probably embarrassed to let anyone know that his father was an invalid and unable to coach!

And then Steve said quietly, "My father said he'd coach us."

The words hung in the air a moment,

thickening the silence. And then everything shattered as a loud, happy shout exploded from the boys. Chris felt his heart melt, and he threw his arms around Tex.

"Oh, boy! Finally!" he cried.

"Well, at least till you get another coach," Mr. Herrick said.

The boys looked at each other, their faces shining with a glow that Chris hadn't seen in a long time. Another coach? Now that they had Mr. Herrick why would they want to look for another one?

"Well, let's get cracking," Mr. Herrick exclaimed, taking a pencil and pad out of his shirt pocket. "Is all the equipment here?"

Chris was staring at him — and thinking hard. Something was nudging at his mind, causing a bubbling inside him.

"Well?" Mr. Herrick grunted, his eyes sweeping the boys.

"Yes, sir, it is!" said Chris, his heart pounding.

"Fine," replied Mr. Herrick. "As soon as the Pipers get off the field, take over. We're scheduled to take our raps last."

He looked around at the boys, all of whom were just standing about, thrilled that at last they had found a new coach.

"Hey, what is this?" he shouted. "A picnic or a baseball game? Play catch! Warm up! The picnic's over!"

Chris smiled at Tex. "We've got ourselves a coach!" he cried.

He wanted to say something else, but Tex was running off with a ball, eager to play catch and loosen up his throwing arm.

12

THE FIRST THING Mr. Herrick did was change the lineup. He shifted Chris to second in the batting order and Wally to sixth. He also shifted Frank Bellows from eighth position to fifth and started Don Mitchell at right field instead of Spike Dunne. Don was eighth in the batting order. Bill Lewis was pitching.

"Batter up!" yelled the ump.

The sky was gray and there was a light breeze blowing. The stands were packed.

The first Piper stepped into the batter's

box and Bill Lewis stepped onto the mound.

"Play in closer, Tex!" yelled Mr. Herrick. Chris looked over at third and saw Tex take a few steps in closer toward the basepath. *Now that's coaching,* he thought happily.

A blast over short! Then a bunt to third that Tex fielded nicely and pegged to second. A wide throw! The runner raced to third and the hitter to second.

"Watch your throws, Tex!" shouted Steve.

Tex was hurt. You could tell by the way he kicked at the dirt.

"Tough luck, Tex!" said Chris. "Get the next one!"

A long, shallow drive over second! Both runners scored, and the hitter came to rest on second base. A clean double.

The next Piper drove a hot grounder to Chris. He fielded it and pegged it to first for the out. A grounder through short scored another run. A strikeout and a fly to center fielder Mick Antonelli ended the Pipers' big inning.

"All right. Now it's our turn," said Mr. Herrick. "Tex! Chris! Steve! You're the first three hitters!" He lowered his voice. "Now, listen. I don't know if Coach Edson ever gave you any signs, but I will. Two's enough. When I touch the brim of my cap, that means the batter bunts. But the runner must make sure the ball is on the ground before he takes off. Understand?"

The boys nodded.

"Good. The other sign is for a hit and run. I'll give it only when a man's on first and only in certain situations. That sign is crossing my arms. Got it?"

The boys nodded again.

"Fine. Okay, Tex. Start it off."

Tex did, with a walk. Chris glanced at Mr. Herrick and saw him touch the brim of his cap. The bunt sign was on.

He let the first pitch go by. It was high. The next pitch was in there and he laid it down. A clean bunt to third. The Piper third baseman threw him out at first, but Tex was safe on second.

Steve flied out to short left, bringing up Mick. The cleanup hitter singled through second, scoring Tex, and Frank grounded out.

Pipers 3, Blazers 1.

The second inning went scoreless, but the Pipers came back hot again in the top of the third, again scoring three runs.

"They're hitting Bill pretty hard, Dad," said Steve as he came in to the bench.

"Okay. So now you fellas hit Keller hard," responded his father.

Chris grinned. Invalid or not, Mr. Herrick was acting as a real coach should.

Tex, leading off again, banged out a single. Chris expected a bunt sign from Mr.

Herrick but the acting-coach was looking in another direction. *Had he forgotten?* Chris wondered. *Should I bunt, anyway?*

He did.

"Foul!" yelled the ump as the ball arced back to the screen.

"Chris!"

Chris saw Mr. Herrick motion to him, looking rather disturbed, and he ran to the bench.

"Did you see me touch my cap?" asked Mr. Herrick.

"No. I thought you'd forgotten."

"No, I didn't forget," answered Mr. Herrick. "We're five runs behind. This is no time to bunt. Get up there and swing!"

Chris belted the third pitch for a single, advancing Tex to second base. Then Steve doubled, scoring Tex, and Chris held up at third. Mick grounded out and Frank poled a long one to center. The fielder caught it.

Chris tagged up on the catch and raced home for another run. Wally walked and Jack Davis grounded out to end the half-inning.

Pipers 6, Blazers 3.

Neither team scored again till the bottom of the fifth when, with one out, Mick tripled to deep left center and scored on Frank's single over second. Spike Dunne, pinch-hitting for Wally, flied out. Then Ken Lane, pinch-hitting for Jack Davis, got on base by virtue of an error.

"Bring 'em in, Don!" yelled Chris as Don Mitchell stepped to the plate. Don took a couple of mighty swings, then popped a fly to the pitcher to end the threat.

The top of the sixth. The last inning. And the game looked dark as ever for the Blazers. Having Mr. Herrick coach the team helped a lot, but he couldn't *hit* for the Blazers; he couldn't *catch* for them. He could only advise what to do. It was up to them to do it.

Crack! A long, streaking belt to deep center field. Mick dropped back . . . back . . . and caught it! One out.

Another long drive! A clean hit to left center going for two bases. A hit now would put the Pipers ahead by three runs.

Bill Lewis pitched hard to the next batter, got him to a three-two count, then struck him out. The next Piper socked a sizzling grounder to Chris. Chris got in front of it, missed the hop, and the ball hit his chest. He quickly retrieved it and fired it to first. Out!

"Nice hustling, Chris," said Mr. Herrick as the second baseman ran in to the bench. "Now let's get some hits."

Bill, leading off, struck out. Tex belted a long drive to center, but to no avail. The Piper outfielder caught it on the run. One more out and that would be it. The Blazers would go down to their fourth defeat in a row, twice at the hands of the Pipers.

Chris liked the pitch coming in, swung and *crack!* A hard, shallow drive to right center. He rounded first and made it safely to second for a neat double.

Steve hit a scratch single, advancing Chris to third base, and Mick came up.

"Over the fence, Mick!" yelled Chris. They needed a long blast to tie the score, a homer to win the game.

Crack! A blooping fly over third! Chris scored and Steve held up at second.

Pipers 6, Blazers 5.

Two more runs. They needed two more.

Frank was up. So far he had grounded out, flied out, and hit a single. *If you're ever going to do it, Frank, do it now,* pleaded Chris.

Wham! A real hard, solid blow to deep

116

left! The Piper fielder dropped back . . .
back. . . . He couldn't reach it! The ball
dropped behind him, both Steve and Mick
crossed the plate, and Frank stopped at
third for a beautiful triple — a triple that
won the ball game.

It was over, and the Blazer fans screamed
their throats dry as they swarmed onto the
field and hugged the players who had come
through for them.

Then Chris, Tex, Steve and the rest of the
team advanced upon Mr. Herrick like a
horde, and one by one they shook his hand.

"Mr. Herrick, please coach us the rest of
the season, will you?" asked Tex. "We need
a guy like you."

Mr. Herrick smiled. "Well . . . I don't
know," he said modestly. "Some of you
didn't like a stranger telling you what to do."

The place went silent all of a sudden. The

boys looked at each other, then at Mr. Herrick. And then, like a shot, the realization hit them.

"You're the man on the telephone!" Tex yelled.

"That's *right!*" the other guys chimed in, all except Chris.

Mr. Herrick's smile spread wider and he nodded. "Right. I'm the man on the telephone," he confessed.

"I thought you were," Chris said. He turned and looked beyond the backstop screen and the grandstand, to the white house catercorner across the street, the house where the Herricks lived. He looked back at Mr. Herrick.

"You watched us from your house," he said. "That's how you knew us and were able to tell us what we were doing wrong."

Mr. Herrick nodded. "Yes. I was using

119

binoculars and I had Steve give me your names. That's how I was able to call each of you."

Chris turned to Steve. "Did you know he was doing it?"

"Yes. But I didn't want to ask him to coach the team. I . . . I didn't think you guys would . . . well . . . want him to."

"Oh, no?" cried Chris. "What about it, guys? Do we or don't we want Mr. Herrick as our coach?"

"YES, WE DO!" they shouted almost in one voice.

"There," said Chris. "It's settled."

He smiled at Mr. Herrick. "Thanks, Mr. Herrick," he said. "We really appreciate it."

"So do I," replied Mr. Herrick, smiling and blinking his eyes. "And from now on call me Coach."